AFRO  I'm Gonna Be

D1482475

By Wade Hudson
Illustrated by Culverson Blair

Printed in the U.S.A. First Edition 10 9 8 7 6 5 4 3 2 1
Library of Congress Catalog Number 92-7200
ISBN: 0-940975-40-8

JUST US BOOKS
Orange, New Jersey
1992

"What are you gonna be when you grow up, Stef'?
An athlete?" asked Robo.
"You're always playing with a ball."

"Maybe," answered Stef'. "Maybe not.
Do you know what you want to be?"

"Of course," Robo replied confidently.
"I know what I'm gonna be."

"I'm gonna be a doctor like
Dr. Daniel Hale Williams.
I could discover a cure for a terrible disease."

"I might be an astronaut like Dr. Mae C. Jemison.
I could be the first person to visit Mars."

"Maybe I'll be a chemist like Dr. Percy Julian.
I could make new medicines to help
sick people get better."

"Or, I could be an inventor like Elijah McCoy. I'd invent machines to make work easier for everyone."

"Well, I know what I'm gonna be
when I grow up," said Glo'.
"I'm gonna be a movie director
like Spike Lee.
And my movies will win
lots of awards."

"Maybe I'll be a choreographer like Katherine Dunham.
I could create a new style of dance."

"Or, I could be a music composer like Mary Lou Williams. I'd write hit songs for Michael Jackson, Whitney Houston and for orchestras, too."

"I could also be a public relations director like Terrie Williams. I could help the stars develop good images for the public."

"Excuse me, Glo'," said Stef'. "Maybe I won't
be an athlete. Maybe I'll be a businessman and own
my own company like Reginald Lewis. I can give jobs
to many people in my community."

"Or maybe I'll be a police officer and become police commissioner like Willie Williams."

"I could be a diplomat, too, and help settle disagreements between countries.
I could be just like Ralphe Bunche."

"Or I could be a publisher like John Johnson. I'd publish popular magazines."

"A physicist is what I plan to be," said Tura. "I could be like Shirley Jackson. Maybe I'll find new ways to explain how things work in the universe."

"What if I become a psychiatrist
like Dr. Frances Cress Welsing?
I could help people find answers to their problems."

"But I know I like to draw and construct things. I could be an architect and design beautiful buildings like Paul R. Williams."

An engineer would be great, too. I could be
like Archie Alexander. I could plan and
build important bridges."

"I've always liked to take pictures,"
said Nandi. "I could be a photographer like
Lorna Simpson and photograph many
important events."

"Perhaps I'll be an artist like Elizabeth Catlett,
and have my paintings shown all around the world."

"But I like talking to people, too.
Maybe I'll be a newscaster like Norma Quarles
and report the news to thousands of people."

"On the other hand, maybe I'll be a designer
like Lois Alexander and create many new fashions."

"Actually, I've thought about being a politician," said Langston. "I could run for the office of pres[ident] of the United States just like Jesse Jackson. I'd win, too!"

"Or, I could be a writer like Langston Hughes. I already have a lot of ideas for stories."

"My dad said I would make a good lawyer.
I could be like Constance Baker Motley and
win court cases that would help all people."

matter what we decide to become," said Nandi,
have to study hard and always do our best."

d never give up," cautioned Robo.

"Yeah," added Langston, *never* give up."

A NOTE TO OUR READERS

Have you ever thought about what you want to be when you grow up? There are so many occupations from which to choose. Here are short descriptions of the ones mentioned in this book. They are followed by brief profiles of the people who chose them as careers. Find out more about these occupations and the people who decided to pursue them. Ask your parents or a teacher to help you.

Artist one who is skilled as a sculptor, painter, potter or who is accomplished in other forms of art. Artists may have their work displayed in homes, offices, galleries or other public places. Artist **Elizabeth Catlett** was born in 1919. Her work can be found in museums around the world.

Architect a person who designs buildings and other large structures. **Paul R. Williams** was a renowned architect who designed many buildings and homes in California. He also designed the memorial at Pearl Harbor. He was born in 1894 and died in 1980.

Astronaut a person who is trained to fly in a spacecraft. An astronaut explored the surface of the moon. Others have performed scientific experiments in space. **Dr. Mae C. Jemison** was the first African-American woman selected to be an astronaut. She was born in 1959.

Athlete one who has chosen sports for a career. Many consider **Michael Jordan** to be one of the greatest athletes playing in the National Basketball Association. **Zina Garrison** is among the best professional tennis players in the world.

Businessperson one who owns or manages a company or a business. **Reginald Lewis** is one of the most successful businessmen in the world. After helping to establish the first black law firm on Wall Street, he initiated a "leverage buy-out" that led to his heading one of the largest corporations in the world, TLC Beatrice International Holdings.

Chemist a scientist who works in the field of chemistry. Chemists work everyday to create new medicines to help treat illnesses and to develop new substances and products. **Dr. Percy Julian** helped to create drugs that are used to treat glaucoma, an eye disease, and also medicine that is used to give relief from the pain of arthritis. He was born in 1898 and died in 1975.

Choreographer a person who creates a special set of steps and movements that others can perform. Choreographers create dances for movies, dance companies and television shows. **Katherine Dunham** was one of the first choreographers to introduce African and Caribbean rhythms and movements to America and the world. She was born in 1910.

Diplomat a representative of a government who conducts relations with the government of other nations. In 1950, **Dr. Ralph Bunche** became the first African American to receive a Nobel Peace Prize. He helped to negotiate a peace settlement in the Middle East in 1949. Dr. Bunche was born in 1904 and died in 1971.

Doctor a person who is trained and licensed to treat diseases, injuries and to perform many other functions to help heal people. There are many kinds of doctors. **Dr. Daniel Hale Williams**, a surgeon, performed the first successful heart operation in 1893. Dr. Hale, who was born in 1856 and died in 1931, also established a hospital in Chicago.

Engineer one who plans and builds structures such as bridges, canals, oil wells and tunnels. **Archie Alexander** engineered and built the Tidal Basin Bridge in Washington, D.C. He was also once governor of the Virgin Islands. Alexander was born in 1888 and died in 1958.

Fashion Designer one who creates the look and style of fashions or clothes that people wear. The designer **Lois Alexander** has been called the "griot of Black fashion." She established the Black Fashion Museum in 1979 to recognize and to house rare items designed and sewn by African Americans. She also helped to establish the Harlem Institute of Fashion.

Inventor a person who thinks up new ideas or who creates new devices and methods that help make life easier for others. Inventors created the computer, television, telephone and the VCR. **Elijah McCoy** was among the first African Americans to receive a patent for his inventions. The self lubricating machine, which he developed in the late 1860s, helped industries around the world. McCoy was born in 1843 and died in 1929.

Lawyer   a person who is trained to give legal advice to people and to represent them in court. Lawyer **Constance Baker Motley** argued nine successful cases before the United States Supreme Court for the NAACP. The legal battles she has won have made a big difference in the lives of millions of people. Motley is now a chief judge of the Federal District Court that covers parts of New York State.

Movie Director   a person who supervises and guides the performers and technicians in the production of a film or movie. **Spike Lee** is a movie director whose films focus on various aspects of African-American life. Among his films are "She's Gotta' Have It," which he financed himself, "Jungle Fever," Mo' Better Blues," and "Malcolm X."

Music Composer   a person who creates music and puts it into a structure so it can be performed by others. **Mary Lou Williams** composed many songs for jazz and classical orchestras and ensembles. Her compositions were performed by such jazz greats as Duke Ellington, Louis Armstrong, Benny Goodman and Andy Kirk. Mary Lou Williams was born in 1910 and died in 1981.

Photographer   one who makes a living taking, selling and sometimes exhibiting photographs. These photographs may be used in newspapers, magazines, books or shown on television, in art galleries or homes. In 1990, at the age of 30, Lorna Simpson became the first black woman to have her photographs exhibited in the Venice Biennale in Italy and the first to be given a solo exhibition in the Painting and Sculpture department of the Museum of Modern Art in New York City.

Physicist   one who works in the field of science called physics. Physics deals with energy and motion. In 1973, **Shirley Ann Jackson** became the first African-American woman in the United States to earn a Doctorate in Physics, which she was awarded from the Massachusetts Institute of Technology. She specializes in solid and condensed state physics.

Police Commissioner   a person who oversees the police department of a city. As police commissioner of Philadelphia, **Willie White** planned policies and devised strategies that helped to make the city a safer place in which to live. Because of his success in Philadelphia, he was selected to serve as chief of police in Los Angeles, California.

Politician   one who holds or seeks an office in local, state or federal government. In 1984, **Jesse Jackson** became the first African American to launch a major campaign for the highest office in the land—president. He sought the office again in 1988. Many people believe his efforts will make it easier for an African American to be elected president.

Professor   a teacher of the highest rank in a college or university. As an educator and president of Morehouse College, **Dr. Benjamin Mays** inspired and encouraged thousands of students. Among those he influenced included the civil rights leader, Dr. Martin Luther King, Jr. Dr. Mays was born in 1894 and died in 1984.

Psychiatrist   a medical doctor who treats disorders of the mind. **Dr. Frances Cress Welsing** is a child psychiatrist. She served as assistant professor of pediatrics at Howard University. Dr. Welsing is the author of several books, including *The Cress Theory of Color-Confrontation and Racism* and *The Isis Papers*.

Public Relations Director   one who works to develop a good public image for a person or a company. **Terrie Williams** established her own public relations agency in 1988. Her agency has represented such stars as Eddie Murphy, Bobby Brown, Sinbad, Dave Winfield, Jackie Joyner Kersee and "Take 6."

Publisher   one who produces books, newspapers, magazines or other printed material to sell to the public. **John Johnson** is founder of one of the most prosperous African-American owned publishing companies in the United States. His company began with *Negro Digest* in 1942, followed by *Ebony* in 1945. Other publications include *Ebony Man* and *Jet*.

Television Newscaster   a person who delivers the news on television. **Norma Quarles** began her career as a television news reporter in the 1960s when few African Americans were seen on television news programs. During her career, she has been a reporter, producer, news correspondent and a news anchorperson.

Writer   a person who creates stories, poems, novels or plays for others to enjoy. **Langston Hughes** was one of America's most outstanding writers. His work realistically depicts the life of African Americans. He wrote poems, plays, stories and lyrics for songs. Langston Hughes was born in 1902 and died in 1967. He is considered by many to be the dean of African-American literature.